For Oscar Belfrage Bordoli ~ M.M.

For Fay B. with love ~ M.McQ.

Text copyright © Miriam Moss 2005
Illustration copyright © Mary McQuillan 2005
First published in the United Kingdom in 2005
by Hodder Children's Books, a division of Hodder Headline Limited,
338 Euston Road, London, NW1 3BH
First published in the United States of America by Holiday House, Inc. in 2005
All Rights Reserved
Printed in China
www.holidayhouse.com
First Edition
1 3 5 7 9 10 8 6 4 2

Library of Congress Cataloging-in-Publication Data
Moss, Miriam.
Bare bear / written by Miriam Moss; illustrated by Mary McQuillan.—1st ed.
p. cm.
  Summary: When a strong wind snatches Busby's clothing off the line, the little bear begins
searching and, with help from his friends, finds his clothes in the most unexpected places.
ISBN 0-8234-1934-7
[1. Clothing and dress—Fiction. 2. Bears—Fiction. 3. Lost and found possessions—Fiction. 4.
Stories in rhyme.] I. McQuillan, Mary, ill. II. Title.
PZ8.3.M84665Bar 2005
[E]—dc22
2004054364

Bare Bear

by
Miriam Moss

illustrated by
Mary McQuillan

Holiday House / New York

Busby, a small, brown
bouncy, young bear,
lived deep in the mountains
in a neat little lair.

One night as he slept
a stormy wind blew,
snatched his clothes
off the line...

and away they all flew....

When Busby woke up,
he cried, "That's not fair.
My clothes have all gone;
I've got nothing to wear!"

Busby looked in the garden,
then in the wild wood,
and there stood a hare
in a red riding hood!

In her basket she carried
a checked cloth,
a fruit flan,
and a small ginger cake
to share with her gran.

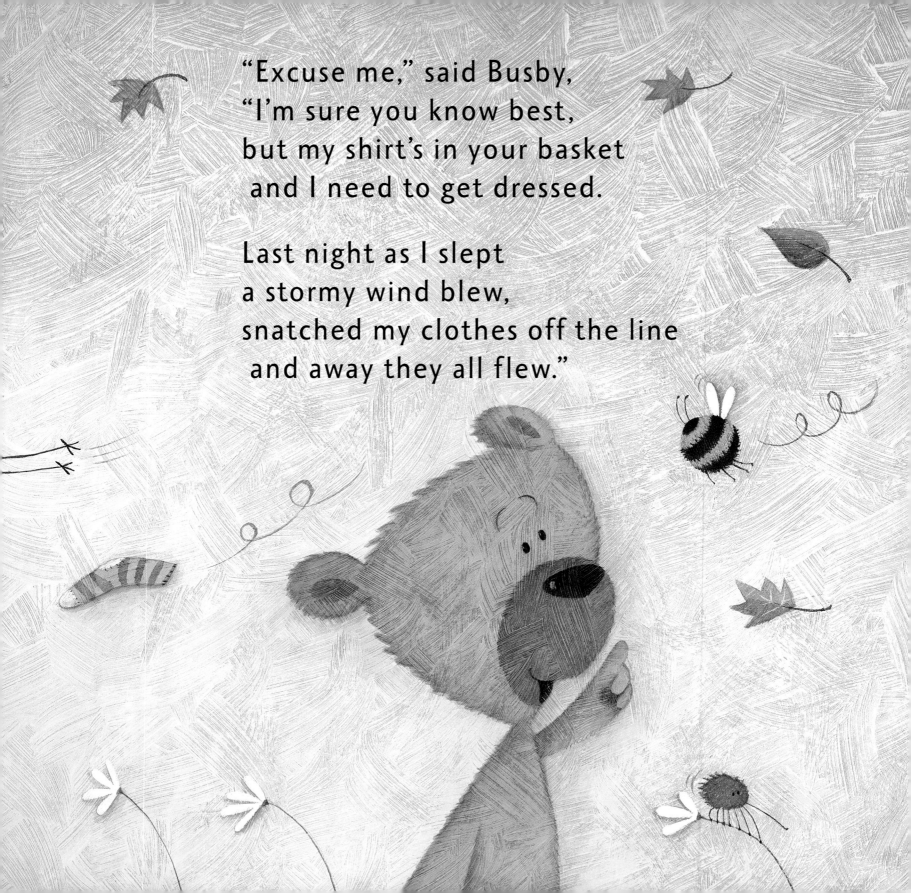

"Excuse me," said Busby,
"I'm sure you know best,
but my shirt's in your basket
and I need to get dressed.

Last night as I slept
a stormy wind blew,
snatched my clothes off the line
and away they all flew."

Hare held up the cloth.
"Yes, I see you're undressed!
You *are* short of clothes.
Let me help find the rest."

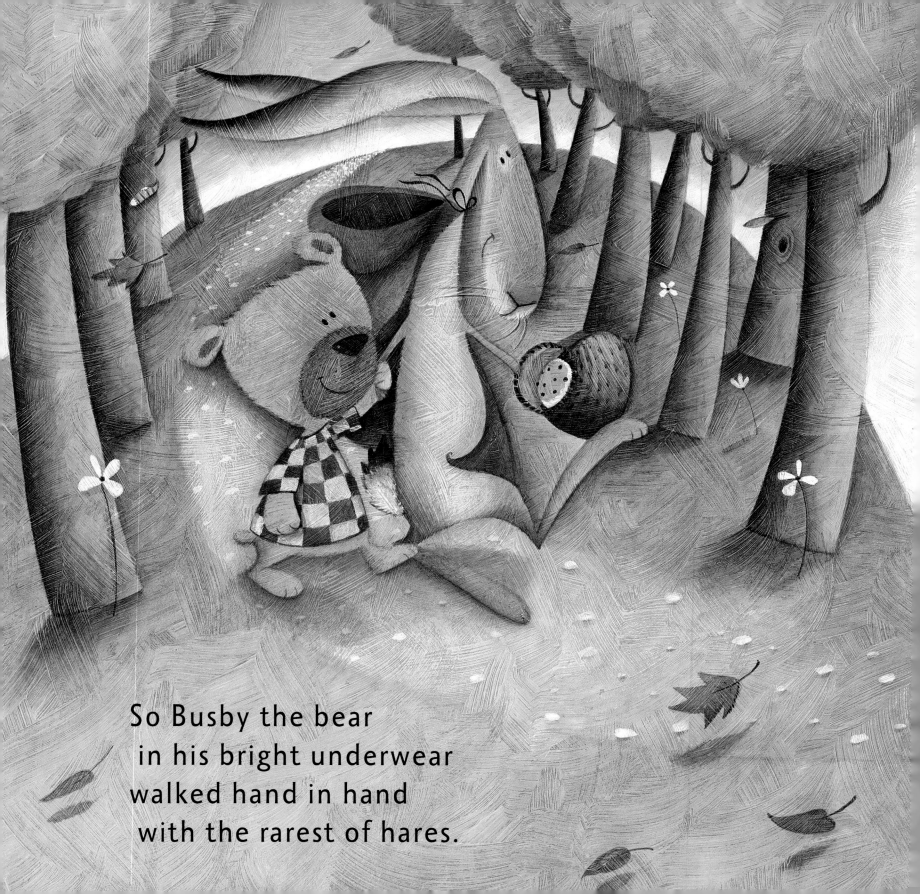

So Busby the bear
in his bright underwear
walked hand in hand
with the rarest of hares.

They searched high and low.
They looked everywhere.

They walked in a circle
and then in a square....

BOING! BOING!

Leaning out of a house
that was clearly a clock
was a mouse who was holding
a striped yellow sock.

Then he started to use it
to polish the clock!

The clock went TICK
TOCK

as the bear went KNOCK
KNOCK!

and the mouse he ran down
to unfasten the lock.

"Excuse me," said Busby.
"I think that it's time
to mention right now
that THAT sock is

MINE."

Mouse held up his duster.
"Yes, I see you're undressed!
You *are* short of clothes.
Let me help find the rest."

So the rarest of hares
and the mouse from the clock
walked hand in hand
with the bear in one sock.

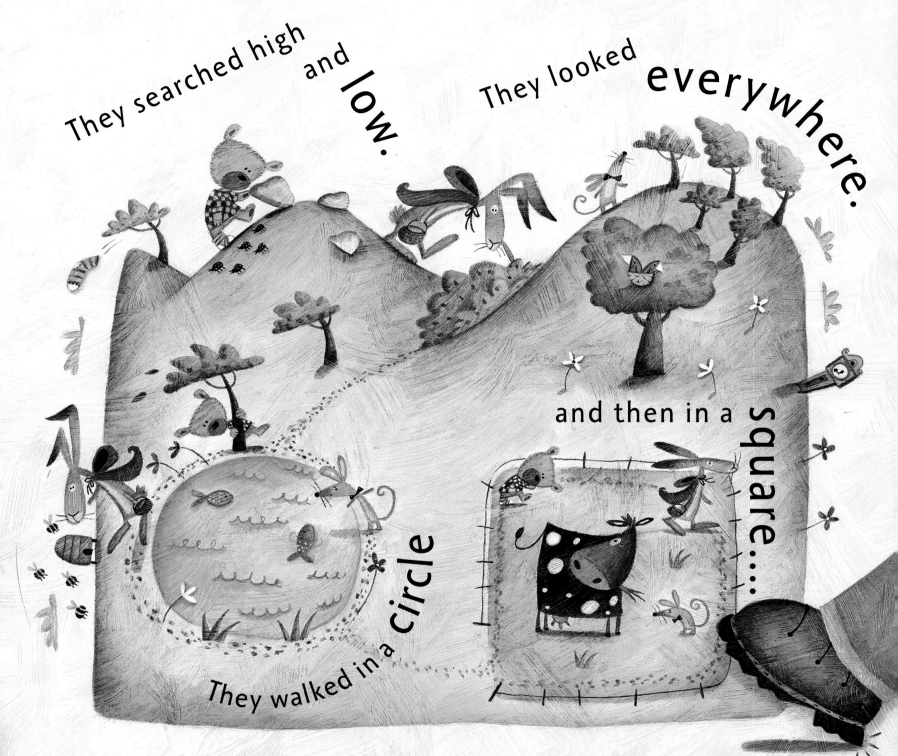

They searched high and low.

They looked everywhere.

and then in a square....

They walked in a circle

"FEE! FI! FO! FUM!"

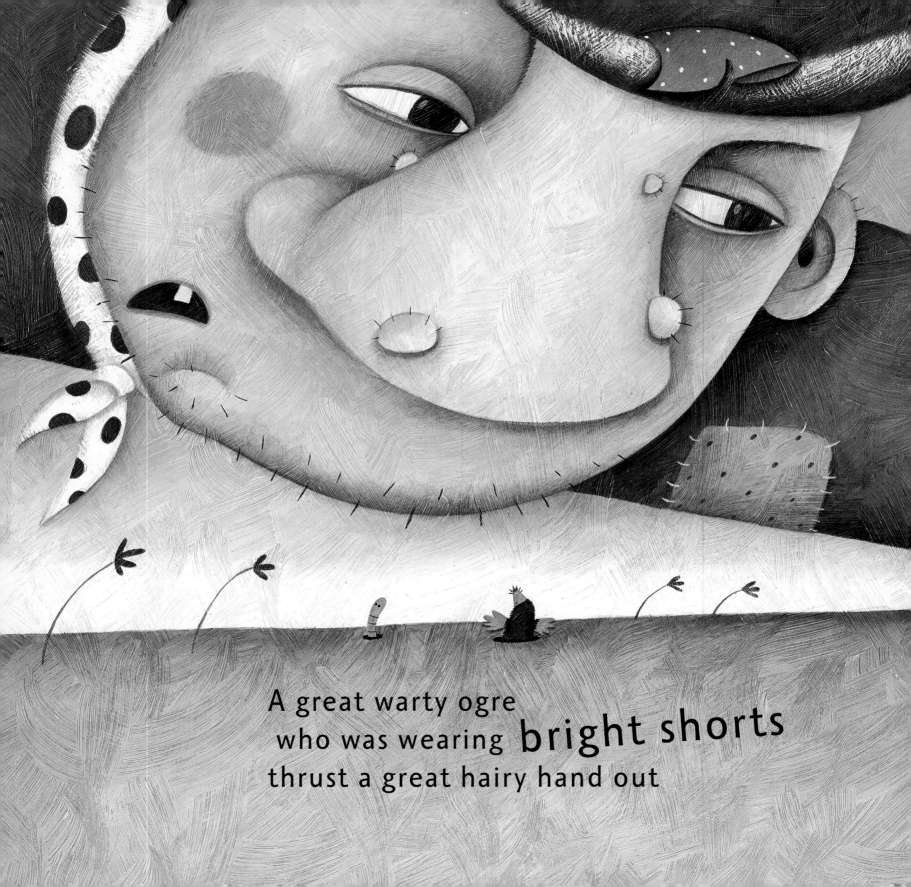

A great warty ogre
who was wearing **bright shorts**
thrust a great hairy hand out

and—HELP—they were caught!

Oh, how they all trembled
as they hung in midair
while the ogre stared hard
at the mouse, hare, and bear!

"Thank you," squeaked Busby,
now down on the ground.
"It's so good to know that
we're safe and we're sound.

I hope you won't mind,
or feel out of sorts,
but stuck to your hat
is my lost pair of

shorts."

So the hare and the mouse
and the ogre with warts
walked hand in hand
with the bear wearing shorts.

They searched high and low.   They looked everywhere.

They walked in a circle...

...and were back at bear's lair!

Busby opened the door
and was in for a shock,

because there by his shoes
lay one striped yellow sock!

Busby tied up his laces
and smoothed down his hair,
saying,

"Thank you, my friends, now
I'm not a bare bear!"